PECAN PIE
Baby

Jacqueline Woodson

illustrated by Sophie Blackall

PUFFIN BOOKS
An Imprint of Penguin Group (USA) Inc.

Just as summer started leaving us and the leaving brought all those colors to the trees, Mama pulled out my winter clothes.

"Time to give away the stuff that's too small," I said. "This didn't used to be a *mini*-dress."

Mama smiled. "Let's keep it, Gia."

And I knew what was coming next—more talk about the

ding-dang baby.

"I don't know why we have to keep my old stuff," I said.
"You do too know why," my mama said back. "Because there's going to be another baby coming soon."

"Not *real* soon, right?"

"Probably by the time the first snow's on the ground," Mama said. "Cool, huh?"

"Not very," I said.

I looked out at the falling leaves and made a silent wish for
winter to come and go quickly without bringing any snow.

Mama touched my hair. "I'll tell you one thing. This baby
sure loves itself some pecan pie. It's wanting some right now."

"Well," I said. "I love pecan pie. And you love pecan pie.
So that baby's just being a copycat!"

In the kitchen Mama cut us a big slice.

By the time it was jacket weather, everyone was talking about that baby!

"You want a boy or a girl?" my friends Juna and Omi asked at recess.

And my friend Trixie said, "Let's play Mama's Having a Baby."

When my friend Micaela slept over, she said, "Your mama better not put that baby in *my* bed, right? Because then, where would I sleep?"

Man! I was thinking. That **ding-dang** baby's going to try to take the place of my sleepover friend!

Even my aunties were baby crazy. When they came over for our weekly Sweet Tea and Toast Party, they both drank their tea in one huge gulp and ate their toast in two bites without either one of them saying to me, "Why, isn't the weather marvelous, dear Lady."

Then they got up and sat with Mama, talking about that baby.

All fall the leaves kept dropping off the trees and the days got shorter and shorter.

One Saturday, a huge box came, and all afternoon my uncles were in my room, scratching their heads and fussing with each other as they put that baby's crib together.

At school, my teacher read a book about a girl who was
going to become a big sister, and when she finished reading it,

everybody looked at *me*.

When my cousin came to visit with her new baby, she put the wiggly thing in my lap and said, "You sure are ready to be a big sister, aren't you?"

"Not really," I said, handing the crying baby back to her.

One night, Grandma took us out to a fancy restaurant.
She kept fussing over Mama. "Eat your greens," she said.
"And you should order some brussel sprouts for the baby."

Mama made a face and we laughed.

"Uh-uh, Grandma," I said. "It's not a sprouts baby. That
baby loves pecan pie."

So for dessert, me and Mama shared a piece.

"Are you getting enough rest?" Grandma asked. "You
know I can take Gia. That baby needs you now."

I wanted to say, *I need Mama now.*

Then Mama reached over and rubbed my back. "Me and
the baby need Gia with us."

And even though I didn't like it when Mama talked about
that **ding-dang** baby, her hand felt nice on
my back and I was glad that she needed me.

Some days I sat on my stoop thinking about all the years it had been just me and Mama.

About us drinking hot chocolate and telling silly stories.

About the mornings I jumped into her bed when it was still blue-pink outside, snuggling up to her while she tried to keep on sleeping.

Now, that baby was going to change everything!

When my cousins came for Thanksgiving, all anybody could talk about was baby this and baby that.

"I'm so sick of that ding-dang baby," I said.

But I guess I didn't say it loud enough, because everybody kept laughing and talking and making plans for when the baby got here.

The whole table got quiet.
And Mama sent me to my room.

Upstairs, I got that teary, choky feeling. And even though there were a whole lot of people in my house, I felt real, real,

real alone.

Later on, Mama came upstairs and sat beside me.

I didn't look at her.

"You know what I'm going to miss the most when the baby comes, Gia?" Mama asked.

"I know what *I'm* going to miss the most," I said. "My whole, whole life, before . . . before the . . ."

"Ding-dang baby," Mama said.

I smiled. "Yeah. Before that ding-dang baby."

"Guess what," Mama whispered.

"What?" I said.

"I'm gonna miss that too."

"For real, Mama?"

"For real."

"Those were the good old days," I said.

Mama smiled. "Guess you're going to have to tell the baby all about it."

I nodded. "I guess I am."

Then Mama hugged me and we sat like that, just being all cuddly, with that ding-dang baby jumping around in Mama's belly. After a while, Mama said, "It's cold out there tonight. Weatherman's calling for snow."

"Then let's go downstairs and eat some dessert before that ding-dang pecan pie baby gets here!"

Mama laughed. Because she knew, just like I did, how much the three of us loved ourselves some pecan pie!

For Toshi Georgiana and Jackson-Leroi, of course   —J.W.

For Ria and Skyler   —S.B.

PUFFIN BOOKS
An imprint of Penguin Young Readers Group
Published by the Penguin Group
Penguin Group (USA) Inc.
375 Hudson Street
New York, New York 10014, U.S.A.

USA / Canada / UK / Ireland / Australia / New Zealand / India / South Africa / China
Penguin Books Ltd, Registered Offices: 80 Strand, London WC2R ORL, England

For more information about the Penguin Group visit www.penguin.com

First published in the United States of America by G. P. Putnam's Sons,
an imprint of Penguin Young Readers Group, 2010
Published by Puffin Books, an imprint of Penguin Young Readers Group, 2013

THE LIBRARY OF CONGRESS HAS CATALOGED THE G. P. PUTNAM'S SONS EDITION AS FOLLOWS:
Woodson, Jacqueline.
Pecan pie baby / Jacqueline Woodson ; illustrated by Sophie Blackall. p. cm.
Summary: When Mama's pregnancy draws attention away from Gia, she worries that the special bond they share
will disappear forever once the baby is born.
[1. Pregnancy—Fiction. 2. Mother and child—Fiction. 3. Single-parent families—Fiction. 4. Babies—Fiction.]
I. Blackall, Sophie, ill. II. Title. PZ7.W868Pec 2010 [E]—dc22 2009047515
ISBN (hardcover) 978-0-399-23987-8

Puffin Books ISBN 978-0-14-751128-7

Printed in the United States of America

10

The publisher does not have any control over and does not assume
any responsibility for author or third-party websites or their content.